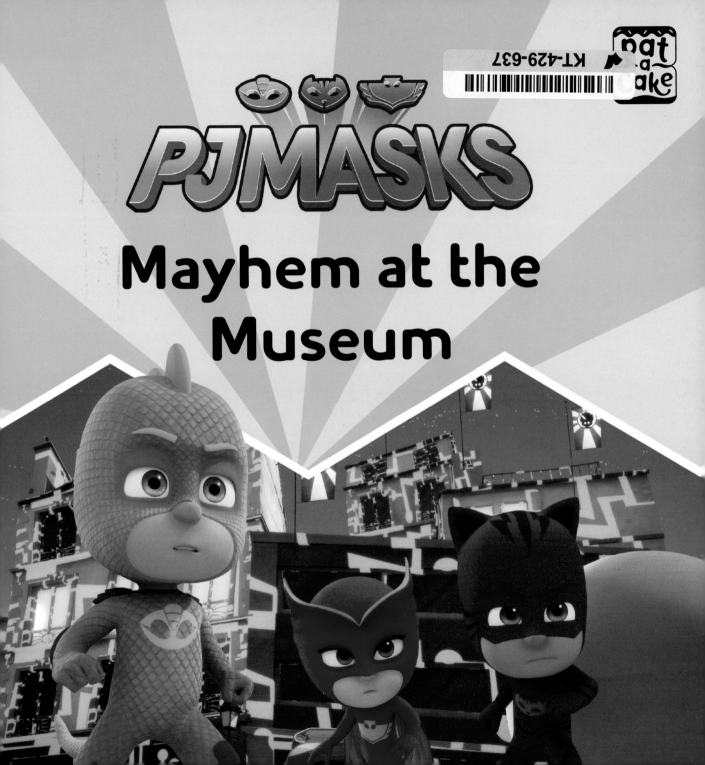

PJMASKS

Mayhem at the Museum

It was the start of science class and the children were building model rockets. Greg couldn't wait.

"I'm going to make the best rocket ever!" he told Connor and Amaya.

Greg rushed up to collect his supplies.

"Oh," he said. "There are no more paper towel rolls. I can't make a rocket without one."

"Maybe you'll get a new idea on our trip to the science museum?" said Connor.

The teacher shook his head.
"I'm afraid the trip is cancelled. The power has gone out at the museum."
Connor frowned. The PJ Masks needed to check this out!

PJ MASKS ARE ON THEIR WAY, INTO THE NIGHT TO SAVE THE DAY!

NIGHT IN THE CITY. A BRAVE BAND OF HEROES IS READY TO FACE FIENDISH VILLAINS TO STOP THEM MESSING WITH YOUR DAY.

AMAYA BECOMES . . . OWLETTE!

CONNOR BECOMES . . .

Owlette put the museum up on the PJ Picture Player.
"Look!" she cried, pointing at the screen.
Gekko blinked in surprise. "That's Romeo's Lab! Let's go after him!"

The PJ Masks set off in the Gekko-Mobile. There wasn't a second to lose! Soon the heroes were zooming towards the museum. Romeo was standing outside, looking very pleased with himself.
"What are you up to?" shouted Catboy.

Romeo puffed out his chest.

"I've taken over the museum while I finish my Big Box of Bad!" he bellowed.

"What's that?" asked Owlette.

"The Big Box of Bad has the power to turn the city into my own private town," the villain boasted.

"No way!" shouted Gekko. "We're coming inside!"

Dooiiinnnngg!

Romeo had set a booby trap so, when Gekko tried to come close, the ground sprung up beneath him. The hero was sent spinning into the air. Owlette and Catboy caught him just in time! "I've booby-trapped the entire museum," laughed Romeo. "There's no way you're getting in here."

"We have to get inside," said Gekko.
Owlette thought about Romeo's booby traps.
"Instead of going in," she argued, "maybe we should try and get Romeo out?"

The PJ Masks made a clever plan. They knew one thing that would lure the baddie out of the building – ice cream! The heroes played a tune that sounded just like an ice-cream van.

Romeo dropped his screwdriver and scuttled outside.
"He's coming!" whispered Catboy.
Gekko jumped out of his hiding place. "Got you now, Romeo!"

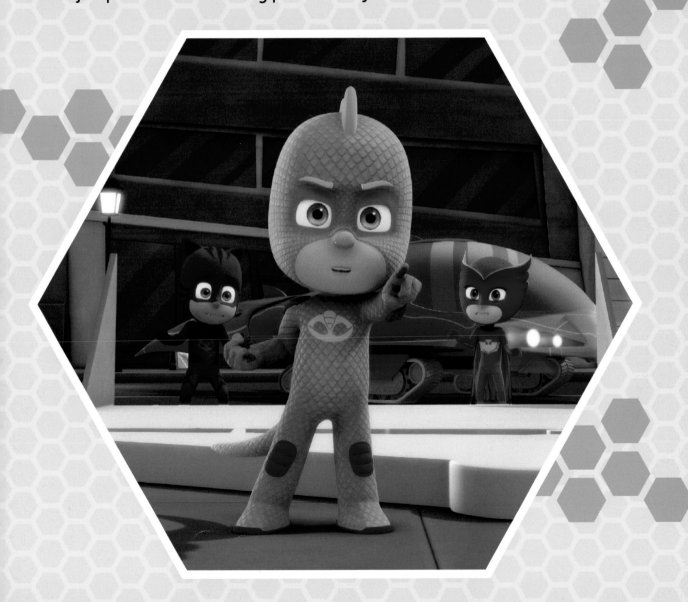

Romeo stood in the doorway,
glaring at the PJ Masks.
"I really wanted ice cream," he scowled.
"I'll make you pay for this!"
Gekko dashed towards the museum steps.
"Super Lizard Grip!"

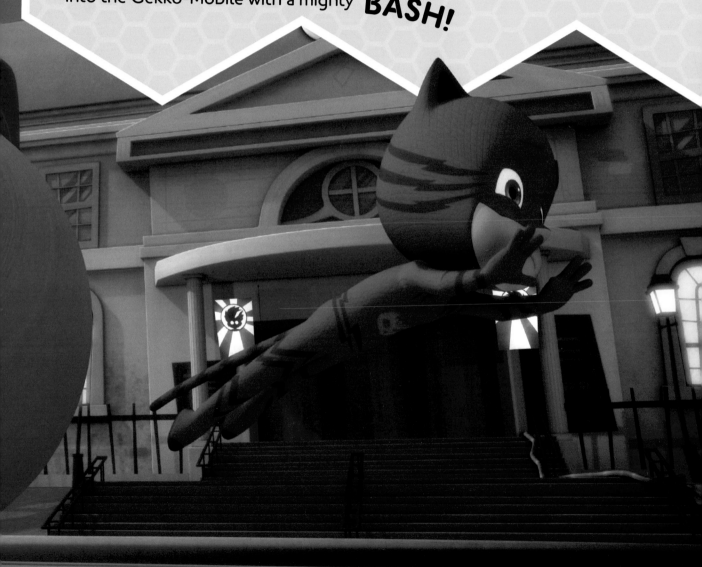

"You PJs never learn," said Romeo, ducking back inside.

"Gekko!" shouted Catboy. "Watch out!"

A giant ball rolled down the museum roof . . . straight towards Gekko! The hero jumped on the ball and ran. The ball rolled faster and faster, before crashing into the Gekko-Mobile with a mighty **BASH!**

The PJ Masks needed to think again.

"Follow me," said Owlette. The heroes climbed onto the museum roof. Catboy lowered a cheese down into the room below. "This will stink Romeo out of the museum," he whispered.

It didn't take long for the baddie to sniff the cheesy whiff.

YUCK!
I need some fresh air!

Gekko spotted the villain trying to escape.
"I've got you now, Romeo!" he shouted, leaping into view.
But the baddie pressed a button. Jets appeared, blasting
the PJ Masks with Super Duper Smelly Spray! Ew!

The PJ Masks jumped away from the stinky smell.
"Gekko," said Owlette, "there's more than one way to solve
a problem. We can't keep running in after Romeo, it's not working."
Catboy nodded. The heroes needed to try again to get Romeo
out of the museum.

"Mwa ha ha!"

Romeo and his robot helper marched onto the museum steps. "I've finally finished my Big Box of Bad!" he announced, cackling with glee.

The villain's new invention began to whirr and light up. Flags popped up on buildings across the city. They all showed Romeo's grinning face.

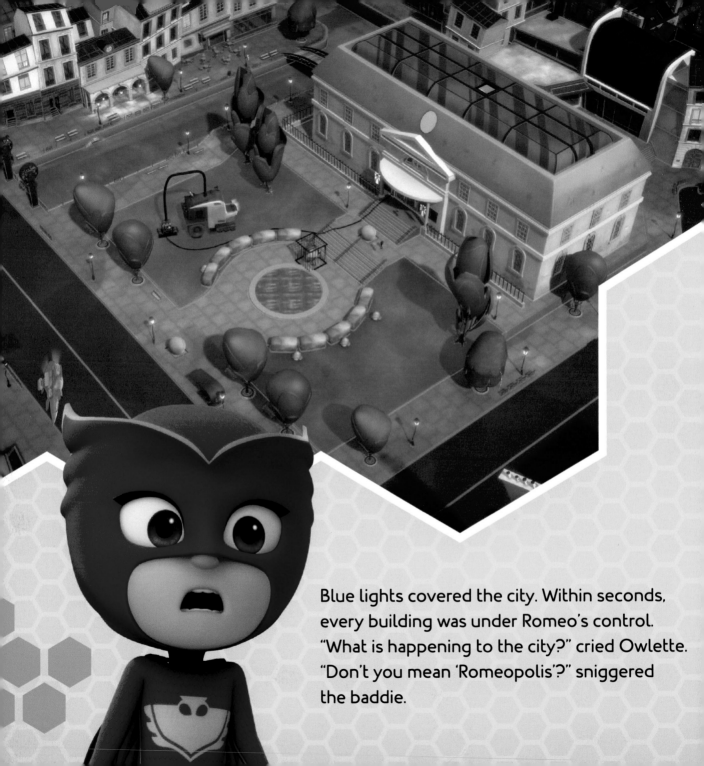

Blue lights covered the city. Within seconds, every building was under Romeo's control. "What is happening to the city?" cried Owlette. "Don't you mean 'Romeopolis'?" sniggered the baddie.

Gekko felt sad. This was all his fault!
"If I hadn't been so focused on doing
things one way, Romeo would never
have finished his Big Box of Bad," he said.
The villain disappeared back inside
the museum, slamming the door
behind him.
"We're never getting in there now,"
sighed Catboy.

Gekko spotted Romeo's Lab parked in front of the museum.
It was time to be a hero!
"Follow me!" he shouted.

Romeo looked outside. His Lab was zooming around in circles!
"My Lab is moving?" he gasped. "That's impossible!"
The villain ran up and jumped into the driving seat. The Lab stopped.

Gekko waved up at the window.
"I was moving it," he grinned, "with my **Super Gekko Strength!**"
Gekko had used his hero skills to make himself invisible. Romeo had been tricked!

Romeo jumped out of the Lab, but the PJ Masks were one step ahead of him. He made a dash for the Big Box of Bad.

"Master," warned his robot helper. "Remember the . . ."

"BOOBY TRAPS!"

yelled Romeo, as one catapulted him into the air.

Romeo was caught in his own cage. A giant ball rolled onto the Big Box of Bad, crushing it into a thousand pieces.

"The plan worked!" cheered Owlette. "The city is back to normal."

"I'll get you next time, PJ Masks!" roared Romeo.

The next day, Greg had another go at making his rocket.
Romeo's Big Box of Bad had given him lots of brilliant ideas.
"Like it?" he asked.
"Love it!" said Amaya.
Greg held the model up. "I call mine . . . the Big Rocket of Amazing!"

PJ MASKS ALL SHOUT HOORAY.
'CAUSE IN THE NIGHT, WE SAVED THE DAY!